For mighty Christopher
—AH and JH

Library of Congress Cataloging-in-Publication
data is on file with the publisher.

Text copyright © 2016 by Ann Hassett and John Hassett
Pictures copyright © 2016 by John Hassett
Published in 2016 by Albert Whitman & Company
ISBN 978-0-8075-3003-0

Printed in China
10 9 8 7 6 5 4 3 2 1 LP 24 23 22 21 20 19 18 17 16

Design by Jordan Kost

For more information about Albert Whitman & Company,
visit our web site at www.albertwhitman.com.

Goodnight Bob

by Ann and John Hassett

Albert Whitman & Company
Chicago, Illinois

"Goodnight Bob," said Moon.

Bob saw two eyes.

It was Fish.

"Goodnight Bob," said Fish.

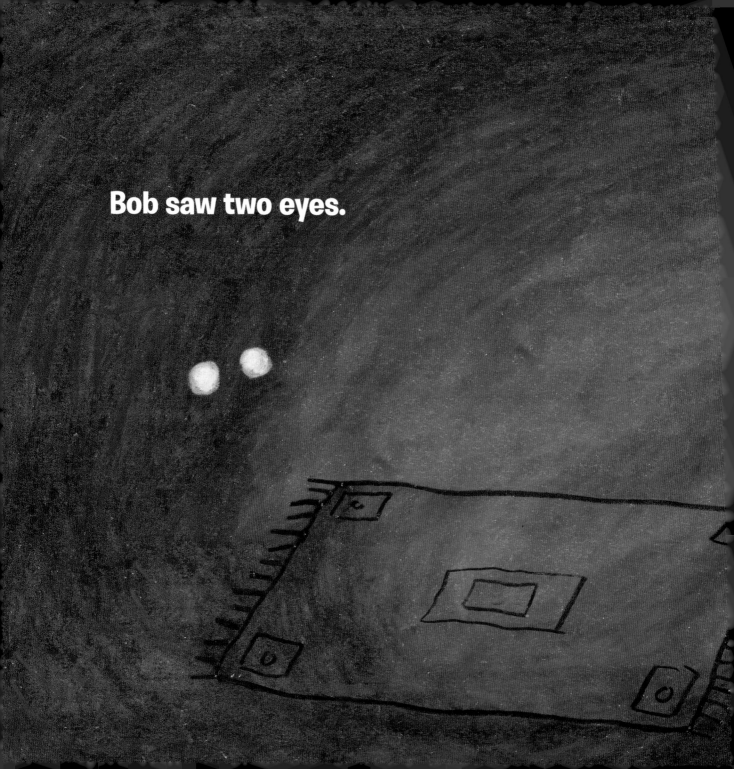

Bob saw two eyes.

It was Cat.

"Goodnight Bob," said Cat.

It was Dog.

"Goodnight Bob," said Dog.

Bob saw two eyes.

It was Mouse.

"Goodnight Bob," said Mouse.

**Bob saw two eyes
at the window.**

It was Bigfoot.

"Goodnight Bob,"
said Bigfoot.

Bob saw lots of eyes.

It was Stars.

"Goodnight Bob," said Stars.

Bob closed his two eyes.

Goodnight Bob.